WINNIE THE SCROOGE

Benjamin Egbert   Michael J. Egbert

This book is dedicated to A.A. Milne and Charles Dickens who inspired me to write this story and rhyme. Thanks to my family, too.

~Benjamin

Table of Contents

<u>STAVE 1</u>

In the Beginning

For a time, the city of London stood as a beacon to the world. A symbol of excellence, to which every other society has attempted to duplicate. Amidst its towering cathedrals and decadent palaces, the city possesses a certain type of allure beckoning all to come and see its splendor.

Oddly enough, behind every cobblestone alley and gated garden lies a secret which most choose to ignore. This city runs on money. Not just pounds and pence, but the wealth of the world has changed hands in this very city a time or two. That sea of money is the bedrock of this great place.

It's impossible for a soul such as I to account for every farthing ever spent. Sure, managing money has a certain connotation associated with it. The feelings towards someone burdened with such responsibilities can be eschewed as negative. Still, I implore you to consider this: if it wasn't for someone like me, who's to say that house around the corner would ever be built. That park on the other side of the street, it's probably gone.

Money lender, a miser. Sure, I'm labeled such things because I'm willing to make the necessary sacrifices to get the job done. If not for me, every Tom and Chelsea would be asking for a handout. Such panhandlers are accustomed to looking for an emotional creature who's susceptible to their pleas. Well, that's not me. I'm about the business of doing business.

Any possible semblance of compassion left me long ago. Why, Rabbit Marley and I saw an opportunity in this crumbling old city. When we first arrived, the London air carried a rotting stench. It was unmistakable.

As we scouted different offices, we realized how meager the city appeared. Sure, near the Thames, there may be a house here or there of some worth, but who wants to stay in a city where manure is more prevalent than a flower. I mean, it's one thing to climb out of a carriage and step into it, it's another to walk the streets knowing that every creature has carried that same waste some distance. Fragments of such matter are spread from end to end and no one seems to care.

Well, Rabbit and I cared. The idea of allowing our paws to walk in another's waste is abhorrent. Immediately, we went about securing as many investors as we could. Assuring them that we had their best interests in heart.

Our plan was simple. If we bought low, we could make the necessary repairs to the investment causing a more selective set of dreamers to return to the city. Their preference would be to choose our homes over some shabby place near Canary Wharf.

Pretty soon, every creature wished to stay in one of our properties. It was easy enough to transition our business away from acquisitions and into lending. Afterall, every esteemed family wished to 'board our ship'. They could see that Rabbit and I were going somewhere.

Well, the months turned into years and the years turned into decades. It was last spring that fate became inevitable. My partner, Rabbit, was going to die. I watched him grasp for any straw that would allow him to live. Yet, death came knocking at his door. By summertime he was gone. His absence forced me to take on an apprentice.

Kanga is capable enough. Although, she lacks a certain vigor which I'm accustomed to. About every two weeks, she attempts to sway me on one of the accounts we manage. I could tell how each patron's pleas pricked her gentle heart.

Oh, how I miss Rabbit. He saw the world in the way any good Brit should: fulfilling one's duty. Ours was to elevate the life of all Londoners. We were the caretakers of wealth while also providing a higher standard of living for others. It's a real shame that he's gone.

You see Christmas is here and everywhere I go it's *Mr. Scrooge this* and *Winnie that.* Honestly, I've never liked my name. Besides, what kind of mother names her son a girl's name? Winifred! Bah humbug! I've thought about changing it a time or two, but doing so would destroy the one person who brought me to life.

I know that I've grown up and am old enough to change my name to whatever I want, but I'm afraid doing so would ruin me. Afterall, everyone in London knows my name, Winifred Alistair Scrooge. Unfortunately, my birth name is not the one I hear spoken by those in hush whispers. That name has taken on a meaning of its own. To most, I'm known as Winnie the Scrooge.

How clever of my patrons to use my first and last name as a label. Scrooge! That name has its own designation. Somehow, my last name has come to mean a person who's both loathsome and lacking in compassion.

Still, the one person in my life who disputes such a designation is Kanga. I'd like to believe her affection towards me comes from a place beyond her salary. Then again, how would I know. She's dependent on me as her employer to provide a sustainable source of living.

I offer her ten pounds a week. It may not seem like much, but I have a responsibility to my investors to not be frivolous with their money. They're counting on me to grow their investments. If not, they'll find a way to take it all back and entrust it with someone else.

I know being frugal isn't in vogue now a days, but when I walk the streets where we've invested and see the change from what was to what is, there's not a grander feeling than being the one associated with accomplishing something so remarkable that all the Lords and Ladies of the Court come to me, seeking my assistance.

Can you imagine, me, 'Winnie the Scrooge' entertaining Dukes and Duchesses. Before I left home, I was told that I had very little brains. That I was some sort of silly bear, worth nothing to no one. Yet, here I am and the world is waiting to see where I go next.

I may not have much in terms of material possession and those I once considered an acquaintance have gone the way of the dodo, but what I do have is a legacy built upon my work. There's very little someone could add to it that would take away from what I've already done.

My only wish is that Rabbit would have lived long enough to see what we've done. Actually, have a chance to witness what we accomplished. I kept thinking that thought during his funeral, that and why so few mourners were there.

Afterall, Rabbit told me he had a great many relations. Sure, he never saw them, but he's family. You'd think they'd mourn his departure.

If not them, at least some of our tenants. Maybe even an investor. I would think his contribution to their current wealth would be reason enough to pay their respects. Still, no one came. That is, no one except me.

I watched my friend get buried in the corner of the cemetery, near a gorse bush. Although not intended, I felt that bush had an uncanny resemblance to the nature of my friend. Ever sharp and not one to toil with.

Oh Rabbit! I could have used you on a day like today. For a week or so, many of our patrons have come to our door issuing requests for the firm to forebear on our arrangement. Why, I remember the time we first started and was naive enough to take someone at their word. Who was it? Jordan? No, it was Ernest!

Ernest offered us the purest of pleas. We obliged his request only to find out that he delayed his payment to account for his family's obligations towards Christmas. Well, you could imagine poor Rabbit's thoughts. For someone to lie so blatantly, risking everything we were attempting to do.

You may rest assured that neither of us has made that mistake again.

Yet, here's Kanga. A hard worker, but ignorant to the plights of others. Her discernment is a nuisance. Each day she approaches me, attempting to sway me from my position. Her fragility is moving. There was a moment or two when I almost gave in to her petitions.

Thankfully, my logic is sound and my rationale is well-established. Although Rabbit is gone, I continue to carry his name in our work. Every day, I weigh whether I'm doing enough to keep our investors committed to our cause. Besides, it's not my money I'm collecting, it's theirs.

I may view things differently if I were the sole benefactor to the firm. In whatever case, I'm not. What's mine is theirs. Those things that are theirs are not mine. The last thing I would want to do is ruin whatever connection I possess to the pool of investors which we've accumulated.

It's the day before Christmas and I've already been stopped three times on my way to the office. It's always someone from somewhere wanting me to give them what is not mine to give.

Sure, I have a few shillings of my own, but what's mine is mine. I worked hard for it. What reason would I have to give it to another? To displace my monetary means to a soul incapable of profiting from it, what a waste of an investment.

What's given will be spent. The best case would be if the peddler that received my assistance used the means as a way of obtaining a decent meal. By all measures, it's more likely that I'd find my kindness spent at the end of a bottle.

I'm afraid, without Rabbit, I'm stuck in isolation fending off the hoards attempting to rob me of my cupboards. If only Kanga could see things the way we saw them. I'm sure everything would be different.

It's at this moment that I swore I could hear a light tapping coming from the other side of our door. I peeked over my desk, hoping to find a shadow or something that would signify a presence hiding behind the old oak.

I waited, but nothing. I returned to my work, when again a sound reverberated from the door. This time, much louder. I ordered Kanga to see who was making such a fuss.

At the turn of the handle, a meager creature stepped into my office. I immediately recognized the shape of the figure, it belonged to my nephew Piglet. Such an insecure lad. I told my sister she babied him too much.

Look at him, weak at the knees and in the spine. I've never known a male species to behave in such a way. Whenever I see him, I'm convinced he's not an Englishmen, for what sort of Englishmen fidgets so relentlessly?

After an initial gaze, I'm required to remind myself that as an adopted child to a childless woman, he would be smothered. Fearful of anything because she babied him so. Right now, I see that he's fearful of me. Me? His uncle?

Why, I've known the child for most of his life. Somehow, he's straining himself in attempting to ask me the question he's come to ask. I'm sure life hasn't been easy on him since his mother passed away. Afterall, he was never prepared to live on his own.

Rather than wait for his bumbling to turn into a coherent thought, I barked, "Nephew, I see you out and about. What can I do for you?"

Piglet stuttered, "Wwwa, well you see. What I mean is…"

"Spit it out! I don't have all day."

"Sorry Uncle. What I wanted to ask is if you'd like to, what I mean is that I was hoping you'd sort of want to…"

"Piglet! Time is money and you are stealing my time! Get to the point!"

"Sorry, I wanted to see if you'd like to spend Christmas with me?"

"Christmas? Why on earth would we see each other on Christmas?"

Piglet uttered, "Well, Christmas is a time to be with family and you're the only family I got."

I felt sorry for the lad. He was right, I am the only family he has and he's the only family I have. I know losing his mother must be hard on him, but if he was to grow up, now is the time to do it. Rather than cater to his needs, I'm going to do what my sister never would. I'm determined to prepare him for a life on his own.

I issued, "Nephew, we've never spent Christmas together, I see no reason to start now."

Piglet inquired, "Why not? Afterall, Christmas is a time to be with loved ones and I want to be with you Uncle Scrooge."

"I'm sure you'll do fine without me. Go ahead and enjoy tomorrow in whatever way you see fit while letting me keep the day as my own."

"But Uncle, I want you to meet someone. Were to be married and I wanted your blessing."

Marriage? My nephew is getting married. This feeble creature found a woman to wed? I could only imagine the type of person who'd choose to marry someone as insecure as him. I assured my nephew that I had no desire to meet his future bride.

Distraught by my dismissal, Piglet left my office in a hurry. I know I could have been kinder to him, but what good will kindness do in a world such as ours. Kindness does nothing, but expose yourself to the cruelty the world has to offer. No, I'm afraid I took the kinder course of action. At least my nephew will develop a layer of calluses,

shielding him from the harsh realities he'll face without his mother.

Although I was initially disappointed in my nephew's weakness, I've now become fixated on Kanga's demeanor. She seems disturbed, as if what I've done was the worst thing to be done. Oh, how I miss Rabbit.

Regrettably, before Kanga closed the door another guest climbed our steps. The gentleman who entered wore a monocle on his left eye while carrying a cane underneath his right wing. Based on appearance, I thought this feathered being was here to invest in the firm. I was greatly disappointed when he spoke.

He introduced himself by saying, "Mr. Scrooge I presume. My name is Oliver Wilkins, but you may call me Owl. Everyone else does."

Owl? People are so lazy! I'd hate it if everyone went around calling me Bear. Don't they know that a name is the one thing that separates us from each other. I can't very well go around naming everyone that's a boy, Boy, or a girl, Girl. What would distinguish one boy from another?

If I saw this owl amongst other owls, wouldn't they be offended if I shouted '*Owl?*' I thought we advanced our society past the stage of generalizing every creature into specific groups. No, I refuse to call him *Owl*.

That may seem strange to take such a stance, especially when my partner's name was Rabbit. The thing is, that was his name. As ridiculous as it may be, if Rabbit was named a more absurd name, I would still honor his name. In fact, I've been known to call someone Delight. A more appropriate name would have been Dread. Still, Delight is what she was named and so I call her by that name.

I disregarded his suggestion. Offering instead, "No, I think I'll call you Oliver. Now, what can I do for you?"

Oliver must have been used to being called Owl. I could see that he was disarmed by my dismissal. He attempted to collect himself then responded, "Well, Mr. Scrooge, I'm here on behalf of *The Ladies in Waiting Charitable Organization*. We're attempting to collect donations from local businesses to assist some of our more unfortunate citizens during this time of year."

Ladies in Waiting? Who'd name an organization that? What a terrible name? I'm honestly struggling to hear any other word he says because of the abysmal choice in naming of the organization.

First off, what is he doing representing a bunch of women? Shouldn't they be representing themselves? Secondly; isn't a 'lady in waiting' some sort of lackey for ladies of the court. If he's telling me that a bunch of former assistants put this organization together, that'd be one thing, but if this is some high-minded creature of means, then their judgment is suspect to say the least.

The one redeeming notion would be that the organization is meant to emphasize the role of serving. Except, instead of tending to the needs of some Lord or Lady, the organization tends to the needs of the poor. I guess now that I think of it, the names not so bad. Other than the process it takes to figure it out, the name works.

My attention finally snapped back to hear Oliver finish, "as you can see, our charity does a great deal to help the poor."

Honestly, I have no desire to hear him repeat whatever it was that he said. Besides, how can I trust an organization that houses such volunteers who wear so many fine things. I mean, look at me. I don't get labeled a *miser* for nothing. I build fortunes and I'm choosing to wear rags, at least when compared to the value I bring to others.

Afterall, how could I trust someone with money who's developed a liking to the finer things this world has to offer. Who's to say my money will go where he says it will go. No, I'm afraid I've indulged him long enough.

I offered, "I'm sure you feel that it's a noble thing you're doing, but wouldn't it be better to teach someone to fish rather than give them a fish? And if I were to give someone a fish, who's to say how much fish they'll get. It's likely the fish will never reach their lips. No, I'm afraid my money is better suited to nobler causes than your own. I bid you good day. Kanga, will you see our guest to the door?"

Again, Kanga seemed bothered by my behavior. Her disappointment is wearing thin. I directed my head towards the door, urging her to do as I said.

Oliver was stunned, a part of him wanted to yell, but he looked as though he didn't know what to say. Before he went out the door, I heard him shout defiantly, "Merry Christmas Mr. Scrooge!"

I answered, "Bah, humbug!"

Thankfully, the remainder of the day went uninterrupted. I proceeded to review every account that Kanga brought to me and noted which ones were to receive eviction notices. Twenty! That's how many accounts we're foreclosing on. Five less than last year, but still a sizable amount.

Although I prefer avoiding this part of the work, there is a benefit to every property we foreclose on. Every pound that went into the property, remains with the property. It may be a hassle to list the dwelling, but I get to resale it at the same price as before while keeping what was already put in. So, a home of five hundred pounds may, by the end, produce eight hundred pounds. Not a bad way to add to an already profitable business.

I called Kanga to my desk and asked her to file away all the accounts which remained current. While at the desk, she hesitated before asking, "Sir, I was hoping to take tomorrow off."

"What, are you sick?"

"No," she assured, "the thing, it's Christmas and I was hoping to spend the day with my son."

Until this moment, I didn't know Kanga had a son. Oh well, no water off my back. I asked, "Why?"

"Well, it's Christmas and there's not many more I'll have left with him before he's gone. Besides, most people take the day off. There'll be no one to do business with."

Before he's gone? I can't help, but imagine that her boy is of a certain age. He must be getting ready to apprentice somewhere far away. Although I remain irritated by her earlier agitations, I can't help myself. I recognize the wisdom she offers. It's true, what's the point of being here when everyone else is there.

I went ahead and approved her request. Then suggested that she get here all the earlier the next day. Somehow, she found a smile and thanked me. I chose to close the shop early. No point in wasting coal when there's no one there who'll pay for it.

As I stepped outside, I couldn't help, but note how brisk of a night it was. The chilled air forced me to do something I normally avoid. I took my scarf, securely wrapping it around my neck while placing my hands inside my coat.

Normally, I attempt to keep one hand out, in case I come across an unexpected sheet of ice. Not tonight. How could this evening carry such a distinction from another? It's the middle of December and I'm failing to account for a time when I needed to warm myself as much as I do now.

The skuttle around town is that the cold has no influence on me. A convenient narrative designated towards someone whom they've never known. I'm certain their perception of me stems from my indifference to their pleas. I've been known to stand firm on the obligations agreed upon with each patron.

Still, the overarching narrative seems unnecessary. I'm unable to alter the terms of our agreements due to my duty towards each investor. Admittedly, there are times on my walk home that I get lonely. Especially after Rabbit died. The companionship we built was based upon the way we see the world. Our unified perspective is unmistakable.

After turning the corner, I was able to see my home. Strangely enough, I never found refuge here. That peace of mind, connected to every other soul, never found a place within me. Instead, serenity is extended towards me through the process of thumbing sheets of paper. If it wasn't so wasteful in burning the midnight oil, I'd remain in my office throughout the night.

My thoughts were redirected there, recalling the different duties that await me the next day. That's why I was alarmed at what happened next. I reached for the handle to my domicile and fell back when I saw the face of my old partner perched in the spot where the door knocker should be.

I stepped back to rub my eyes, hoping that I was hallucinating. When I came to, I looked and saw that the lion's head remained where it should be. The image of my friend must have been a fluttering thought, brought on by my earlier recollections of him.

I went inside, directing myself towards the wardrobe. Avoiding any delays, I placed my cap and gown on and plopped myself in front of the fire which I stoked moments earlier. As I nibbled on a piece of bread with a spot of honey, I heard a strange sound outside my door.

It was as though chains were being dragged up the stairs. I turned my head towards the source and listened intently as the sound grew louder. Each step seemed to hinder the source's advancement.

Fearing what was outside my door, I went to the fireplace and pulled out the poker. I gripped it tightly,

preparing to lunge the iron into the intruder's heart. Suddenly, the door swung open.

A gust of wind knocked me to my seat. Any thought of fainting was out the window. I now find myself at a disadvantage. As the unwelcomed guest stepped forward, the air became colder, as though the window were opened.

I looked over, hoping that was the case. However, each possible exit remained shut. Again, another gust came forth. This time causing the fire to burn out. What blaze there was is lost in the remaining embers.

I remained speechless as my hands began to shake. Never, not once had I felt so afraid as I did now. I closed my eyes as the intruder dragged himself one step closer.

With my eyes shut, I heard my name. Not surprising when considering this is my house. What shook me was the sound of the voice calling my name. I peeked through my eyelids, hoping to spare myself any physical harm.

Once my eyes adjusted, I could see the figure whose voice matched the familiar sound I heard. Why, it's Rabbit! My partner Rabbit Marley is in my home! Strange. I saw my friend, but not as I knew him. His shape seemed lifeless as if a thick layer of dust had encircled him.

I was in disbelief. He looked the same as I saw him before, but. how could this be? How could my friend be in my home?

Fearful of what came next, I froze. My body stayed motionless in the place I sat. Sensing my hesitancy, Rabbit spoke, "Why Scrooge, don't you know me?"

I uttered, "Your figure is that of someone who's most dear to me, but cannot be, for he is gone. I and I alone watched him be buried near a gorse bush a few leagues from here."

"That you did! And I'm grateful for that. There's something unnerving about watching your body lay to rest, knowing that no one else cared for it."

I pressed, "Watch your body? Whatever do you mean?"

"Oh, I was surprised to see my life end. What affected me most was knowing that it didn't. Before I could move on, I was forced to watch over my body. Awaiting for its final resting place. I'll tell you, finding life after death is not what I expected."

Confused, I stared at my friend measuring his movement. I'm certain the figure before me is him, but I'm forced to doubt my senses. Rabbit perceived my thoughts and counseled, "Fear not, there's nothing inside you causing an hallucination. It is me and I was sent here on your behalf."

"My behalf? Whatever for? It's not like I've done anything wrong."

"I'm afraid Scrooge, there is. We were both led astray."

I implored, "Astray? How?"

"We permitted ourselves to be led astray by the wisdom of the unwise. After I died, I became entangled with a fierce recollection of all my comings and goings. Every encounter with every creature was embedded into my mind. I don't know, maybe it's due to being a specter, but somehow, I relive each encounter. However, this time I'm permitted to see the effects my actions had on others. Oh Scrooge! If you only knew the horrors that waited."

I interrupted, "Horrors! What horrors? I did nothing wrong. You and I did nothing wrong. We fulfilled our duties the way we promised. Keeping that promise is more honorable than any perceived slight we may have caused another. If I offended their nature, it's because they took it that way. They took something that was never intended. Why should I be responsible for their sensitivity?"

"Oh, I'm afraid a simple warning isn't enough for you Scrooge. It'll take a more concerted effort to show you the way. Tonight, you'll be visited three times. Learn what I never could, heed the counsel given. Otherwise, the pains that await you will exceed even mine. Farewell Scrooge."

I called my friend, begging him to stay, but his shadow left me. I sat for a moment, resolute to dismiss my friend's warning. How could I be responsible for someone else's misery? I do what I do because that's what is expected of me. I have the weight of Lords and Dukes depending on me to keep money in their pockets. Achieving such a feat requires a firmer hand on the tiller.

I ignored my friend's pleas by taking myself to bed. I laid there deliberating over the counsel given, then determined it was rubbish. Before I shut my eyes, I muttered to myself, *"Bah Humbug."*

<u>STAVE 2</u>

Looking Back

Sleep has never evaded me. Whether it was warm or cold, loud or quiet, the moment I set my mind to sleep, I found it.

Not tonight. For the first time in a long time, I stayed awake. I tried as hard as I could, but found no sense of weariness. I'd shut my eyes and yet I'm alert. I hear every sound; nothing escapes my attention.

Oh Rabbit! How could you take a night away from me? As the hours wore on, the more I'm convinced that I imagined the whole thing. Visitations, what humbug!

It wasn't until the stroke of twelve that my mind began to drift away. I breathed a sigh of relief knowing that I would find some form of rest. Then, as the clock struck one a bright light filled the room. My curiosity took hold of me. What could be the source powering this exquisite beam?

I opened my bed curtains and to my surprise I found Rabbit standing in front of me. Perplexed, I asked what he was doing here. He answered, ”Why Scrooge, I told you that you were going to be visited three times.”

“Yeah, but I assumed it was going to be someone else. I already saw you!”

“Well, we're on a budget! No point in hiring out when I'm as capable as anyone else to relay the same message. No, I'm afraid I'll be taking you from here.”

I smiled. How couldn't I? Even in death, my friend Rabbit is finding a way to save a penny. Oh, I love how little he's changed. I inquired, “My friend, you seem the same. Do we not change at death?”

Rabbit confessed, “No, I'm afraid we are who we are. Maybe even more so. Life is such a short play and the character we act out stays with us. That's why I'm doomed to the misery I sowed. I continue relishing in the discomfort I caused, yet now I see the effect my actions had on others. There is nothing worse for a soul to experience than to be harrowed up in the memory of your misdeeds. Try as I might, I failed to prepare myself in my probationary state. My scene has ended. I have no final curtain call.”

“Why Rabbit, I never knew you to be such a thespian! You mean to tell me that who I am is who I’ll continue to be? How glorious! I was afraid I'd change in death. Now I have something to look forward to.”

Rabbit shook his head, “Scrooge you are a hard one. I'm afraid this will take all night.”

Suddenly Rabbit transformed into his younger self. Before me is the schoolmate I once knew, but how could that be? Perceiving my thoughts, Rabbit answered, “Our

spirits will always carry those memories of who we are. The ability to portray that version of me to another, let's say I'm getting some help."

Befuddled, I stumbled back into bed. Attempting to ease my mind, Rabbit step forward as the youth he once was and offered his assistance. In his adolescent voice, I heard, "Come Winnie, there's much to see! Take my hand and follow me."

Such encouragement gave me the assurance I needed to proceed. I took his hand and went into the light. When we came forth on the other side, I was surprised to find myself in front of my old school house. Oh, what memories I possessed!

Remarkably, I found myself wandering around, reliving every step of my childhood. My thoughts led me towards the school hall. Upon entering, I was stunned to see my younger self and remarked, "Who's that handsome cub right there?"

"Don't be modest Winnie. If you find yourself attractive then say so. Heaven knows if anyone else will."

""What do you mean? Am I not what I think I am?"

Rabbit corrected, "Of course you are. The thing is, in death, I learned a unique fact about life. Those who pursue good, will do good. Those who seek for the bad will surely find it. If you find yourself handsome, then believe it! Don't wait for the world to convince you so."

I understood my friend's counsel, but my mind was directed elsewhere. I watched my younger self intently as I continually stuck my hand inside a honey pot. Oh, what a reckless wretch I was. Allowing one thing to consume every fiber of my being.

Honey! Oh, how I loved honey! Every second of every day, I was distracted with the thought of it. What were my parents thinking, indulging me as they did? Couldn't they see the harm I was causing myself. Thankfully my school master saw it and worked tirelessly to rid me of my obsession.

It's an odd thing to watch yourself eat. I stood there in the corner of the room closely watching my school master attempt to direct my attention away towards something other than that honey pot. His efforts were futile. My younger self remained committed to the honey in hand, scraping every inch, attempting to claim the last drop. Unlike before, I could see what my spirit possessed then: a

mind bent on salvaging what little was there. Waste not,
want not.

While Rabbit stood next to me, he asked, "What do
you see in yourself?"

"A foolish cub with no discipline."

"How so?"

"Can't you see it? Well, I can. In front of me sits a
fat bear ill-prepared to face the world ahead of him."

"Do you recall what changed in you?"

"I do, but it's something I wish to avoid."

Rabbit attempted to console me by offering, "Come
now, it's time to go."

He held my hand and escorted me into another light.
On the other side was a party of sorts. I adjusted my eyes
and recognized where we were. Why, it's my old employer,
Mr. T. Fezziwig. That silly old creature. No matter where
we were or what we were doing, he insisted on breaking

protocol by having me and Rabbit call him by his first name, Tigger.

Since we were apprenticing for him, we feared to question his reasoning on most things; specifically, his name. Names are a peculiar thing, like time, names have a way of morphing into others. Distorting memories as they were. Now I find myself carrying the same conversation I had earlier, before this whole ordeal began with Rabbit.

I'm torn. I'm beginning to question whether those things I'm thinking now are connected to the earlier dialogue I had or has the rationale always been with me. Afterall, did Mr. Fezziwig's mother think of her son, when naming him Tigger? Who would name a child after their species? And if that was your intent to name him so, then why corrupt the name designated to your kind. At least Rabbit is called Rabbit instead of some distorted alteration like Rab or Bit.

Needless to say, Rabbit could sense my thoughts and asked, "Why does his name bother you so?"

I answered, "Cause that's all we have! Our name distinguishes us from each other and if we're good enough, it'll be remembered long after we're gone."

Rabbit gently smiled which I found to be the most unnerving of sights! I can't remember the last time I saw him grin. He kindly asked, "Well Scrooge, what do you remember about this party?"

"Which party is it? After all, the Fezziwig's threw so many. Oh, how he wasted what little he earned."

"This, my dear Scrooge, is our last. Look, over there."

I turned my head in the direction he was pointing towards and spotted myself in the corner nibbling on another pot of honey. What a disgraceful sight. How could I let myself go?

I watched as I made a mess of things. Right then, another figure entered into my line of sight. It was Abigail! This was the moment we first met. Rabbit placed his hand on my shoulder and pried, "Do you recall what happened next?"

"Of course! Because of her I was determined to set out on my own, to make a living for us both. I think that was the first time we talked of a partnership."

"Your memory serves you well. Not long after, Mr. Fezziwig invested in our business. One of the first to do so."

I smiled, recalling that simple memory, one that seemed to carry so many happier thoughts. I watched my younger self leave the pot behind as I followed Abigail onto the dance floor. I remember how beautiful she was. Beauty may be subjective in nature, but I fiercely admired her.

She seemed to carry herself in such grace. I marveled at the scene unfolding before me. There she was, escorting me around the room, making me feel important, as if I somehow mattered.

It seemed like ages since I relied on that pot of honey for my happiness. A simple tool to mask my misery, yet here was Abigail propping me up for the world to see. Me? I was such a shy bear, who would've imagined it. To finally find something better than honey.

Rabbit pried, "What happened to your obsession with honey? I sort of forgot how much you ate."

"I don't know. If I were to put a little thought into it, I guess the honey pot was a crutch of sorts. You know, something to lean on when I felt down in the mouth. Truthfully, I didn't like depending on it nor the way others looked at me when I did. I think it took this moment for me to put it aside, taking the pot out of my life forever."

"I'm afraid that you never let it go, did you?"

Ashamed by his assertion, I could see that Rabbit gained access to my thoughts and experiences. He took me by the hand, escorting me into another light.

Upon exiting the luster of beams surrounding our bodies, I found myself looking at a slightly older version of who I once was. I could see the calluses forming underneath my weighted eyes. The city of London has a way of turning the softest of bears into the fiercest of bruins. In a month's time, the city will either find a way to spit you out or put you in a corner.

Thankfully, I was given the corner. When I was younger, I was naive enough to believe that I could carve out a large piece of the city for myself. Instead, every maneuver I made solidified the corner I was in. It took years for me to advance further in the city.

However, that moment came later. For some reason Rabbit chose this event. A time in which our firm barely retained any investors. It's at this point my life was at a crossroads. A time which I could have gone one of two ways. Thankfully, I see this moment as the beginning of my ascent.

This little mound is nothing compared to the peaks which lie ahead. For a brief period of time, my life seemed impossible to overcome, yet I did.

Knowing what's ahead, I smiled as I watched myself toil away at my books. Every obligation must be kept. I could never let an account fall into the red.

Rabbit stepped aside, allowing me a chance to watch myself uninterrupted. Although he wasn't near, I could sense that he was studying my thoughts, wanting to perceive my demeanor. I'm afraid he's wasting his time. I can see now what I saw then, I was a bear going about doing one's duty. Keeping up with my responsibilities as they were.

Without warning the door behind me flung open. It was Abigail! She appeared to be out of sorts. For some reason I fail to recall this particular moment. I watched intently as she entered the room. She stood in front of me for some time, patiently waiting for me to notice her.

Like a fool, I ignored her presence, choosing to direct my focus on those tasks at hand. Eventually she coughed, hoping it would redirect my younger self from the work I was so diligently maintaining. Annoyed by my indifference, she attempted to get my attention through a different sound. For some reason, she cawed, which eerily resembled the noise generated by a peacock.

My younger self lifted his eyes just enough to catch sight of Abigail. Like a fool, I went ahead and displayed my contempt for her interruptions. Finally, Abigail had enough!

She ordered, "Winnie! You will hear what I have to say!"

While continuing to look over my books, I saw the indifference I displayed. Not once did I address her directly. Instead, I answered back through a sheet of paper. One that was conveniently placed between us.

I remarked, "Abigail, if I thought what you had to say was worth my time, then I would give it to you. However, I've come to understand that my time is what makes money and it's my time that puts money in the pockets of others. If what you had to say was worth as much as a pence, I'd disrupt my duties to indulge such a remark. However, based on prior discussions, I can only assume that what you've come to discuss can wait until tonight."

For the first time, I could see how my younger self unwound the integral fabric which kept Abigail together. She tried to fight back the tears bubbling to the surface. Rather than give in, Abigail suppressed her tears enough to bark, "Winnie! If you don't talk now, you'll never get the chance again."

"Chance for what?"

"I'm afraid our time has run its course. No matter what I do, I'll never be enough to compete with your fixation on success. I came here in the hope that you'll show some form of affection, but there's no disputing it now. You love yourself far more than you'll ever love me. I think it's time that we go our separate ways."

It's at this moment, which I have a perfect recollection. I watched Abigail leave the office; that was the last image I had of her. In dealing with matters of love, remorse has a way of settling in. It becomes a tool meant to torment participants on the varying actions which they performed, contributing to the outcome they already suffered through.

Thankfully, I've never endured such an exercise of remorse. My entire life has permitted me to evade such discomforts. I count myself lucky. I may well be an ol' miserable bear, but I have a unique gift of separating myself from those types of encounters. I view each relationship, whether friendly or intimate in nature, as a contract of sorts. I was convinced then that I fulfilled the measure of my duties with Abigail.

I could see how I ignored her plights. For me, there was no point dwelling over the mistakes that might've been. If mistakes were made, I shouldn't be held accountable for them.

Unfortunately, the memory of this encounter is failing me. For I see now, what I didn't see then: the harm I caused someone I loved. Until this moment, I genuinely believed the fault lied with her. That the undoing of our arrangement came from her and her alone.

Yet, here I am and can see how little affection I gave her. It's a peculiar thing to alter one's memory. I remember how I felt then, but the memory expanded beyond my own perception. Somehow, I can feel the pain I caused Abigail. My eyes wept as a result of her sorrow.

Rabbit came forth and offered, "Scrooge very few are blessed with such insight. Rather than see the world through their own making, you've been enlightened with a higher understanding of how our actions affect the lives of others. It may be difficult to hear, but the world does not revolve around one single bear, nor twenty rabbits. No, I'm afraid we're all dependent on each other. That our actions are how our lives will be measured for eternity."

I turned to my friend to ask, "You mean to tell me, that what's been done stands as a witness against our existence upon death."

Rabbit nodded, affirming what I feared. If what I feel now is burdened upon me later, how can I survive such torment? The remorse that has long plagued so many, finally has found its place within me. I sensed a steady stream of tears rolling down my face.

Rabbit gently placed his hand on my shoulder, escorting me away from my current sorrow. However, blessed I may be to receive such insight; my soul is weary in dread. I began recounting every action from that point until now and could see my failings along the way. What glimpses of happiness which I once possessed, faded with each memory.

Although I wish to dismiss such proximity to my younger self; sadly, I have to admit that I've become far worse than the wretch I once was. A matted mass of waste, thrown into a corner, awaiting his next line of duty. I'm merely a foot soldier for my investors. It is such a challenge to recognize one's faults, accepting it is an entirely different thing.

So, few see the harm they've caused then witness the effect their choices have on themselves. I can see now what I refused to see before, that I am the miserable miser so many loath. The horrid wretch which others easily detest.

Enough was enough. I pleaded with Rabbit to take me home. Knowing full well the torment caused when acknowledging one's sins, Rabbit sympathized with me, bidding me to follow him home.

<u>STAVE 3</u>

In the Moment

After an initial stir, I found myself back inside my bed chambers. What light there was has since left. I looked around in disbelief. Briefly, I was concerned that someone had slipped me a dose of poison causing such a hallucination.

Whatever excuse I made, the feeling I gained wouldn't leave my side. I was forced to recall the harm I caused poor Abigail. She didn't deserve such a dismissal. Immediately my mind raced through every encounter we shared, causing me to reevaluate each outcome.

Memories are a dangerous thing; pigeonholed into specific narratives, always in favor of the one holding the memory. Based on my prejudices, I saw each argument with Abigail in a new light. In fact, every exchange was brought into question.

Before sorting through each encounter, another burst of light came from the other side of my bedroom door. Frightened by those things ahead of me, I cautiously tiptoed towards the handle, turning it ever so slightly.

With little effort given, the door flung open. The light scarred my eyes for a moment or two. As they adjusted to the sudden brightness, I once again saw my friend Rabbit standing in front of me. Unlike before, there was something different with his countenance. Whatever gloom he once held was replaced with a higher standard of light, as though he was given a new wick, which burned brighter than before.

I marveled at my friend before asking, "Rabbit, you've changed."

"Oh, you've noticed, good! What's the point in doing any of this if you can't recognize the difference in light?"

"Difference? What do you mean, difference?"

"You silly ol' bear! The further we are from the light; the bleaker things get. It's only when we step into the light that we see things clearly."

I pried, "You mean to tell me the only reason I see you this way is because I stepped into the light."

Rabbit dismissed, "No, you've been given a glimpse of the light. For a moment, consider your bed curtains. Their placement on your bedposts is meant to obstruct the light, preventing it from affecting your sleep. The light still exists, but it's you who's blunted its effect. It's you who's chosen darkness. The light you now see is, but a fraction of the light available to you. Come let's not waste the light."

Rabbit took me by the hand, escorting me out of my house. Remarkably, the city of London was about. The night that was is now affixed in the heart of the day. I was puzzled to see such a transition.

As I ventured away from my house, I recognized the faces of those who've long plagued the neighborhood. Oddly enough, they seemed gleeful, even merry as they passed by. I never knew they smiled.

I turned to Rabbit then ask, "What's got them so cheery?"

"Why, it's Christmas Scrooge!"

"You mean it's tomorrow?"

Rabbit corrected, "In a sense, it's today. You've been given the chance to see what today looks like. Unfortunately, most creatures choose to see the world in one of two ways. They either see it for what it once was or what it can be. They never see it for what it is. This condition causes them to miss out on what's happening around them, reacting too slowly to the needs of others."

I challenged him, "I do neither."

Rabbit shook his head, "Scrooge, you may be the worst perpetrator of them all. I've spent the majority of my life next to yours and can attest to your vision. You see neither ahead nor in the past. In fact, your vision is so obscured that you fail to see the forest amongst the trees."

"What the devil are you talking about?"

"You're dwelling on the meaningless prevents you from seeing the effect your actions have on others."

"Meaningless!" I barked, "My life is not meaningless! Nor are my actions!"

"Oh Scrooge, you silly ol' bear! Your life is built upon the conditions which you've set for it. Everything is recorded and balanced in your books. Every transaction is accounted for; nothing is left to chance."

I questioned, "What's wrong with that? There must be order to things."

"Yes, but at what cost?" Rabbit then pointed in the general direction of the crowd. "Are we not their keepers too? You see life only through the prism of those to which you have an immediate obligation towards. Your life is consumed by the agreements the wealthier class has placed on you."

"Did you not also agree to such terms? Were you not equally culpable for these arrangements?"

Rabbit broke. His eyes hid from mine while he admitted the truth of the matter. "Of course I'm responsible for myself. I lived my life and will be judged for what I've done. I must tell you Winnie, there is something splendid, yet horrifying about the capabilities of the soul. I see and remember everything. Not only my memories, but the memories of others. I know the pain we've caused. Come let me show you."

Rabbit guided me to another part of town. It wasn't long before we stopped in front of a tattered old shack. There were holes in the roof along with cracks in the door. Whatever warmth resided inside would quickly disperse,

failing to elevate the temperature of any room within this building.

I inquired, "Why did you bring me here?"

"This is Kanga's home."

"Kanga? My Kanga? The one I see every day? Surely, she could afford a better place than this?"

Rabbit assured me she could not. He mentioned how expensive London's become. As we elevated the standard of living, those of means found a reason to return to the city. Their costs raised everyone else's. There was another fact which eluded my prior grasp, Kanga had a child named Roo.

Roo was once considered an inquisitive child. One that was eager to engage with others. Fearing that her child would fall behind other children his age, Kanga directed her income towards his education. Schooling is such an expense. A liberty only the wealthy can truly afford.

Unfortunately, life finds a way of keeping one in their station. After Kanga lost her husband in the war, she was forced to take care of her son, on her own. Tragically, matters got worse. Roo has been dealing with consumption. The worst of its kind. With her income directed towards his education and the little housing they could afford, there's nothing left to pay for the doctors. As brave as she is, Kanga has long feared this Christmas may be his last.

Rather than share everything with me, Rabbit encouraged me to see what was taking place. I entered the home to find Roo with a warm cloth wrapped around his head. The presence of this child confuses me. I turned to Rabbit to ask, "Who's child is that over there?"

"Mr. Scrooge, he who knows everything, yet perceives nothing. This, my friend, is Roo; Kanga's only child."

"This is the child? Why would she keep such a thing from me?"

Rabbit remarked, "Being a single parent is such a chore. Most employers reject single mothers on the notion they're incapable of attending to their duties. You were not her first choice, nor her tenth. By the time she reached you, she'd learned the art of getting hired *'shut up and keep your head down.'* Isn't that the motto we all strive for. To say and do as little as possible, so as to not ruffle anyone's feathers."

Roo coughed a terrible cough, interrupting our discussion. Concerned for the boy, I pressed, "What's wrong with him?"

"I'm afraid a lot. Consumption has him."

Although my face is capable of displaying several emotions, dismay has never been one of them. A sense of dread came over me. I argued, "Why isn't he with a physician? Doesn't Kanga realize he needs a doctor?"

A sense of shame fell over my friend, Rabbit feared to utter the bitter truth. Seeing the hesitancy within him, I implored Rabbit to finish his thought. Rabbit noted, "She has. She spent all she could on that child and has no more to offer. Every day she leaves him to work for you, fearing that her morning departure will be the last time she sees him. She stays at work because she hopes. She hopes the money she'll make will somehow give her child the intervention he needs. Sadly, the little hope she has in her son's recovery is blunted by the knowledge of his isolation. The torment of knowing that he's gasping for what little air his lungs can carry without her assistance is enough to drive the strongest of souls into the grave. No, I'm afraid the responsibility of being a single mother can wear a soul down to the point of 'no return'."

"You mean to tell me that her choices are: come to work and hope that her child survives while away or stay home and watch him die?"

"In the simplest of terms, yes. She can either attempt to earn what little she makes in the hope of some assistance or she can remain home, where assuredly her employment would have been terminated. Such a decision will only further cement one of two outcomes: she'll either

watch her son die of consumption or starvation. Not the easiest of conundrums to face, is it?"

Roo coughed again. This time a bit of blood remained nestled in the corner of his lips. Right then, Kanga came around the corner with a fresh rag to place on his head. Seeing the worry in her eyes, the child whimpered to his mother, "It's okay mom, really I'm doing okay."

Kanga eyes wore a shade of red, impossible to miss. Knowing the challenges her son faces; Kanga did her best to console her emotions for her son's sake. Roo, seeing the whole affair, remarked, "You know, Jeanie down the street told me that if we truly love someone, they're never really gone. And you love me, don't you?"

Kanga broke down in tears, burying her face into her son's arms. She cried, "Of course son, no mother could love a child as much as I love you. You will always be my greatest gift, my dear sweet Roo!"

Moved by the scene, Rabbit stepped away, leaving me to consider the impact my life has on all of these things. For a bear of little feeling, even I, Scrooge, was moved by Kanga's affection for her son.

As I attempted to reason with myself, Roo uttered, "Mom, make sure to thank Mr. Scrooge. I know what other people say about him, but he's the only one who hired you. There must be something special inside of him that others don't see."

Kanga responded, "You're right, there must be something wonderful."

Rabbit returned, placing his hand on my shoulder, motioning me to follow.

Outside of Kanga's home, I noticed that my friend's presence seemed to diminish. I asked, "What's wrong?"

"I'm afraid my time is up."

I begged, "No, no that can't be! I need you."

"I wish I could stay, but you have one more visit. Regrettably, I cannot be with you."

I attempted a smidge of humor by joking, "What about sticking to a budget? If we're to save money, shouldn't you see me through?"

"You silly ol' bear! Money has no place in death. If you are to heed any counsel of mine, know this; it's the choices and impressions we make in life that follow us in death. No one is perfect, but the burden we place on ourselves is of our doing and no one else's. We, by our choices, impact our salvation. Of course, we cannot atone for what we've done, but the burden you'll come to bear in the next life is unfathomable if you do not strive to improve on the manner in which you conduct yourself. Please Scrooge, I implore you to consider the weight of what you've seen and heed our warnings."

"Our warnings?". A feeling of dismay quickly supplanted what remaining hope I kept as I watched my friend vanish into the shadows.

STAVE 4

What Lies Ahead

Rabbit is gone! He left me to some unknown specter? How could he do this?

I remained motionless, yet my body was taken to another part of London. I was home? Although, something was amiss. As I stood on the street, I could see that it was the same structure I entered into so many times before. However, something was different.

While studying my surroundings, a figure came forth from the shadows. Hoping it was my friend, I stepped forward to greet him. Instead of finding Rabbit, I stumbled upon a creature which I had not known before.

Alarmed by its presence, I muttered, "Wh, wh, who are you? Are you the visitor that my dear friend Rabbit warned me of?"

The figure nodded his head, acknowledging his role as my guide. I attempted to size this fellow up; however, any attempt to do so led me to despair. I couldn't avoid this feeling that whatever laid ahead was filled with dread. My

new companion carried with him an aura that seemed to suck the life out of anyone else.

Without hesitation, I have never met a gloomier or hopeless soul than this one. Preferring to withhold such assumptions, I attempted to engage with him in conversation. Unfortunately, he did not reciprocate my desire to connect. Rather, he took his elongated face and motioned me towards the front door.

Fearing the consequences which may follow if I fail to go as directed, I stepped forward, closer to my guide. Wishing not to offend, I did as any creature would and quickly glanced at the face of my guide as I passed him by. Befitting, my companion was a donkey. A creature, by design, who is meant to carry the labors of so many.

Rather than linger on his appearance, I quickly redirected my eyes towards the door. Once at the handle, I could see that the knocker had changed. My first thought was, *"Surely this couldn't be my house."*

Fearing to reside next to my companion, I continued inside. Structurally, everything was the same. The stairs, along with each room, remained where they should be. However, the furniture that once was, is no longer there. Instead of finding those things that were mine, the house seemed aglow. There was color inside. Especially when compared to my preferred choice in lodging. Each room appeared in a paradisiacal state.

Right then, a lordly fellow came around the corner. He wore a splendid coat with loafers to match. This gallant figure didn't carry himself like some sort of a peacock, more so as a lordly lion. The irony abounds, when considering he's a sheep. My attention remained focused on this creature. Initially, I was upset that he chose to alter my home in such a manner. That feeling went away when I observed how envious I was of him, with the way in which he carried himself.

Suddenly, a group of lambs came rushing in yelling, "Father!"

I watched intently as they embraced their father with such adoration. For a lordly fellow, this ram took each child and showered them with his affection. Assuring that he neglected none of them. As the ram finished doting on his offspring, a lovely ewe strolled into the room.

She eloquently declared, "Why Ramsley, when did you get home?"

Ramsley? Another name to the pile. Anyone wishing to name their son Ramsley, knowing his eventual maturation into becoming a ram, is unoriginal. Oh, his schoolmates must have picked on him something awful. Then again, my partner was a rabbit whose name was Rabbit and my nephew was named Piglet. Such carelessness when naming a child.

Ramsley bellowed, "Why Olivia, I arrived moments ago? I considered exploring the house to uncover its hidden treasures, but my presence was accounted for. Everything fell apart before such an exploration could begin."

"And what treasures you were looking for," she coyishly remarked.

"Why, the greatest treasures in all of Christendom! However, it seems to me that such treasures should not remain hidden." Ramsley walked to the front door, swung it open, and declared, "Bestowed upon me are the greatest gifts known throughout the land! No ram has ever been so fortunate to have been blessed with such a family. I declare my love for them and note their exceptional nature to one and all!"

Embarrassed by her husband's declaration, Olivia pulled her husband inside before he made more of a spectacle of himself. Ramsley remarked, "What? Do you not care for such an acknowledgment?"

Olivia smiled, nuzzling her face next to his, before correcting, "Oh no! I'm ever so grateful for your adoration, but I fear that I need to hide my husband more than he needs to showcase me!"

Ramsley laughed. He loved his wife and her good nature. Before long he asked, "So, my dear. What have you been up to all day?"

Olivia listed a series of duties which were carried out with their lambs before noting her efforts to their living quarters. I took special notice at the mention of the home. Olivia explained, "Well, as you know, the prior owner was not a pleasant fellow. I spoke with Mrs. Jensen next door and she assured me that any dealings of her's with the bear were minimal. She pointed out that everyone did their best to avoid him at all costs."

Ramsley asserted, "No wonder his things were never claimed."

"Precisely! Thankfully, there wasn't much of his that we needed to get rid of. Mrs. Jensen assured me that our lambs are a blessing when compared to the coldness offered by Mr. Scrooge."

Ramsley noted, "Well, you've done a marvelous job with this home. Remember, the gentleman who sold it to us. He noted that no one wanted it because it eerily resembled those catacombs we visited in Paris. I must say, Olivia, you have a gift. To turn this drab cave into a palace of fine art is a wonderment to behold. I think we should explore the possibility of turning your gift into a profession."

"Be serious!"

"I am!" he assured, "Our home will be your centerpiece. I have space inside my office, we can set up shop there."

"What about our children?"

"Look, you've supported me. It's time I support you. That's what marriage is about. Issuing support in each other's needs. Besides, I have space for them to roam around. It'll be great! I promise you!"

Olivia leaped into her husband's arms as he twirled her about the room. As I watched them prance from here to there, a sense of despair came resting on my shoulder. I turned around to see my new companion behind me, looking gloomier than ever.

After receiving my attention, the donkey turned away, motioning for me to follow. I cautiously stepped where he stepped, fearing any personal decision of mine would lead me down the wrong path.

He didn't take long to get us where he wanted to go. Once again, I found myself outside of Kanga's home. Its familiarity was inviting, something which I've longed to feel on a night such as this. I hurried inside, hoping to find Roo on the mend.

As I scurried about the room looking for signs of his condition, Kanga came in carrying a pile of Roo's belongings. Hoping this scene was merely a reflection of a mother caring for the needs of her child, I watched intently to see where Kanga would go.

What I witnessed is not what I expected. Kanga threw those things of her sons into the fire. While watching his clothes burn, she fell to the floor, sobbing in pain. While curled in a ball, she wailed, "Why God, why? My son! How could you take my son?"

I fell into the wall! With my hand covering my heart, I witnessed Kanga's agony. It was too much to endure, so I ran outside, hoping the air would ease my soul.

Neither the air nor my companion were of comfort to me. Instead of offering some solemn condition which would prevent such an outcome, I was taken to a cemetery and placed in front of a headstone. The name carved into the stone is the one I feared, *Sydney Roo Bane.* I covered my mouth in horror, fearing that the remorse I feel would somehow leave my lips. I continued examining the stone, underneath the name was written these words *Here Lies The One Child Who Found The Good In All Beings.*

Startled, I stumbled backwards, tripping over another headstone. I then scampered about the cemetery, hoping to find a way out of this dreadful place. Regrettably there was none. That is, until I uncovered the whereabouts

of my gloomy companion who was looming in the corner of the grounds.

Skeptically, I crept towards him, fearing what horrors awaited me there. Without rhyme or reason, I found enough courage to order, "Spirit, I demand you to tell me what this place is! Is this what will be or what might be? Tell me, is there a way in which Roo could avoid such a fate. Speak to me! I demand you to speak to me! What's the point of you? If you're to be my guide, then guide me!"

The figure said nothing. No matter what commands were issued or threats made, the figure remained where he was.

Fearful of the recourse that awaited me, I attempted to reason with him by issuing, "I understand there's something you want me to see. Afterall, that's what this is about. Opening my eyes, right? I see how my life isn't a stage where I'm the main act. That my existence is intertwined and dependent on others. What I do not only affects me, but those around me. Come now, there must be a reason for all of this. To show me that I can be more than what I've been. That's right, this must have been a chance to show me how I can improve the lives of others, right? That's why I'm here. Sure, that's the reason you refuse to speak with me, so that I can find resolution within myself. Am I right? Tell me! Am I?"

The figure stepped forward and for the first time uttered a syllable. With a bellowing voice, he spoke plainly, "No Scrooge, I'm not here for that. I'm here for this." The figure then motioned with his head towards a burial plot that was isolated from all others, as though everyone preferred a plot away from this one.

I step forward to uncover a headstone which read *Scrooge, Good Riddance*. I stumbled back, nearly falling over myself. The figure explained, "You see, I'm what awaits you. I am what I am."

"And what is that?"

"Death!"

Startled by his admission, I bumbled, "You mean… no, I can't be! That's impossible! Why would you go through such an act without any chance for remission?"

"I'm afraid that's not your decision to make. We are given, but one life and you squandered yours after the pursuit of duty and honor of the world. Look around, there's no one here to mourn you. No one to claim that which you've left behind. Your mark on this world is as shallow as this grave. What life you've made is yours and yours alone. There's only one person responsible for you and you failed yourself. Now, like me, you will have the opportunity to harrow up every misdeed you've issued to another. Come now, let's not waste what little light we have left."

The figure took me by the hand, escorting me to my grave. Fearful of the dread that awaits, I pleaded with him to let me change. In my heart, I could sense that change was possible and assured him that my contrition was real. Yet, he ignored my pleas, urging me to continue towards the burial plot.

As I stepped forward, each recollection of the night's events became apparent to me. Oh, what a fool I was! How could I ever believe that my sum is bigger than the collective whole? How could I conceive that I was an honorable bear when so many moments of honor evaded my attention? Oh, the lives I scarred; the unnecessary pain I caused! Worst of all, Roo!

Roo! That sweet child who was fatherless; desperately attempting to fill the vacant role in his home. Yet life came in the form of consumption and he could not escape it because of me. I prevented his mother from tending to his needs. I kept her away from his final breaths. What sort of monster have I become? Is there no worse pain than the recollection of all the misdeeds which I've done?

If so, I wouldn't wish it upon an enemy! The torment driven by guilt, knowing there were ample opportunities to uplift another is too much to bear. For some reason, I feel responsible for them. As if I were their caregiver and failed to provide care. Even now, Roo's life weighs on my soul. Oh, that sweet child, lost because of me.

Until now, I was unaware of my companion. My mind was so focused on my past mistakes that I failed to account for my footing. The gloomy creature next to me nudged me over the ledge and I fell into the grave.

Immediately, I twisted my body towards him, looking for some explanation of my being here. Sadly, he knew my thoughts. He scarcely moved his eyes when he offered, "Scrooge, I'm afraid this is what awaits you. An eternity of guilt and bitterness. Not towards me nor anyone else for that matter. No, the disdain you feel for yourself remains with you. Your eyes see what you've done and knowledge cannot be unseen. Knowledge is funny that way. You can't unknow something. It sticks with you forever."

Fearing for my soul I begged, "Please, is there no way out of this misery?"

"I'm afraid there's nothing you can do to fix what you've already done."

I offered, "Surely, I can go forward being better than what I've been."

The creature hunched over and whispered, "That's not saying much, now, is it?"

Unfortunately, I knew he was right. If my wallet possessed one dollar then added another, I may have doubled more than what I had, but what I've earned is merely one dollar away from being back where I once started. I knew, if given the chance, my life would not be based solely on the accounting of one bill to another. No, instead my life would need to become an endless pursuit of charitable giving. Acts done out of love, not necessity.

I've never given God much thought, but standing in my grave, aware of all the harm I've caused has directed my attention towards him. There, in my grave, I poured my heart to him. Promising that the life ahead of me will far exceed the one I've left behind.

Tears streamed down my cheek as I cowardly knelt before my maker. As I wept, the blurry figure of my companion went away. Suddenly, I was alone, trapped in my grave. I bent over my knees, clamoring for my soul, when a semblance of strength returned to my frame, I lifted my head to find myself not in the ground, but amongst my things. I was kneeling in my bed.

I looked around. Everything was as it should be, but how? Obviously, I'm home, yet something tells me I'm not. Fearing it was a dream, I knelt down, meditating over what happened. Refusing to let it go, I wrestled over the possibility of it being something more than a dream.

As my thoughts stirred over the night's events, a wonderful notion came to my mind. *Knowledge is not obtained solely by the way of a book, but in what we experience. Those things which we saw and felt.*

Somehow, I knew that the plausibility of all things being real, mattered not. For I saw and felt something remarkable. Whether I was there in a physical form or the night's events occurred within a vision, is irrelevant. I know what I know because that's what I know! I will forever retain the horror I felt from that pain which I've inflicted on others.

I leapt to my feet, pacing around the room. All the while, attempting to figure out a plan of attack. Suddenly, another thought came to mind; *why wait, go and do.*

Go and do is what I did.

STAVE 5

Making Amends

With so many wrongs to right, I rushed out the door wearing my usual waistcoat and top hat. I determined, what's the point of making amends if those I reach out to fail to recognize me. I hurried away looking for my first opportunity to set things right.

Surprisingly, the first family I met; I did not expect. It was Ramsley and his wife Olivia. I don't recall seeing them here before. Such an odd thing to know who the creature will be that'll benefit from your departure. Rather than hold any bitterness towards such an outcome, I was gleeful to see how the pair would benefit and elevate my home. Their presence has left me a bit curious; as if there was some meaning behind their being here this morning. I went ahead and introduced myself.

The pair remained as I remembered them. Lovely and congenial, full of life as they shared their story with me. I remained intrigued on the present whereabouts of their little lambs. As I inquired about the possibility of them having children, Olivia mentioned how there were three, all staying with their grandmother while they searched for employment in the city.

Hurrah, hurray! My first opportunity to demonstrate my contrition. I explained, "Well, I may not have a position at this time to fill, but I'll ask around. I have dealings with other vested individuals who may need some help. As it stands, I do need assistance in one specific matter. Olivia, you see that dreary house over there. Well, that's my home. Clearly, I have no taste and I'd like to make it a more welcoming abode. If I were to hire you, would you be willing to assist me in the matter? You may use my shop as your primary office to work from."

Shocked by the offer, both Olivia and Ramsley fell back in disbelief. After momentary hesitation, Olivia looked at Ramsley, seeking his counsel. He consented with such fervor. She turned to me and graciously accepted my offer. Stunned by the kindness shown, Ramsley insisted, "Sir, I must ask. What name do you prefer to be called by?"

"Well, my name is Winifred Scrooge. Most around here call me Mr. Scrooge, but you're welcome to call me Winnie if you like."

They shook my hand as I issued them the details of my shop and the address of my home. I assured them that the finer points of our arrangement will be ironed out tomorrow. Afterall, it's Christmas morning and they should be with their little ones.

As they turned away, I was reminded of my dear nephew and how cold I've been to him of late. Instead of waiting upon his arrival, I made a concerted effort to find

him. When I did, he was outside his home, tending to his door. He was attempting to hang a reef, visible for all to see.

Startled by my presence, Piglet cowardice away, fearing what scolding I may have for him. I implored, "My dear Piglet, why do shrink whenever I am near? I know I've been a hard bear. A crusty old sinner of the worst sorts. In the past, I thought I was preparing you for the world ahead, I now realize my view of the world was untoward. Unfairly, I laid judgment against the whole of it. I believe now, more than ever, that I wronged you. I am so sorry my dear nephew. You deserved a far better example than I, but I'm here now and I want to become that uncle you deserve."

Piglet was taken back; on a part of my accountability. Without understanding his internal workings, I could see that Piglet preferred affection over correction. He immediately leapt forward and extended his prior invitation to me regarding dining with him tonight. I gleefully accepted, informing him that I had other errands to run, but will return promptly when I'm to be expected.

Although I was grateful for every encounter I undertook that morning, each one seemed to prevent me from reaching my desired destination. I must admit, it's odd to see how affected a soul can be when they're offered a kind word with a smile and a shed of warmth. Rather than skirt away, each creature cheerfully reciprocated my affections towards them by offering the same sentiment.

Still, there is a house I must tend to. No matter the need of the soul, I must press on. Although it took some time, I finally reached Kanga's house. I stood outside reflecting on what I might say. Truthfully, I had no idea what to offer.

Do I apologize for something I didn't know or should I grovel at her feet, acknowledging the courage she's undertaken, enduring such hardships on her own. No, I'm afraid any such attempt would deter from my position of contrition. The last thing I would want to do is to somehow make my apology about me, diluting its intent. There's only one choice left for me to choose and that's to reach out.

So much of our failures occur by wasting opportunities to reach out to one another. This morning alone, I can see how my issuance of good fortune reflected positively within each creature's countenance. There's no point in wasting daylight on the right thing to say when the right time is now.

I knocked ever so gently, fearing that my hammering would alarm her. No need to diminish such a day as Christmas with such coarseness. I waited, but nothing. I fear my knocking might have been too light. I tapped more forcefully, hoping my current efforts would achieve my goals.

Thankfully, there was no need for another pounding. Kanga, came with a smile on her face to greet whoever was at the door. Surprised by my presence, the joy she brought to the door faded when she caught sight of me. I don't blame her. By all means, she's probably concerned that I've come to require her presence at work. She cautiously offered that I join her inside. Doing my best to put her mind at ease, I graciously accepted the offer.

As we stood in her dining area, I could see Kanga fidget, uncertain with what to expect from me. Kanga, knowing that I, the one who came to visit, must have come for a purpose, was on edge, awaiting for my declaration. To ease her concerns, I attempted to remark on the splendid manner in which she kept her home. Truly it was lovely. For having next to nothing, the home seemed full of something which I've never known.

Kanga acknowledged my compliment and assured me that she could do better. Rather than engage with such frivolous talk, I cut to the chase by asking Kanga if it was okay for us to sit a while. She assured me that would be fine.

When I took my chair, I examined the room one last time, hoping that I would see little Roo. Yet, Roo never appeared. Instead of pursuing the whereabouts of her child, I turned my attention towards Kanga and began, "I know seeing me on Christmas is not what you expected, nor what you desired. However, last night, I realized how poorly I've treated you. Poorly may be the wrong word. I think if I were to take account of my actions, my assessment would be that of indifference. I was indifferent to you. Cold and callous. Lacking any sort of feeling. I mistakenly viewed the world through prisms of absolutes. My role as your boss was meant to separate us, keeping me from ever getting to know you. I'm here now to admit how wrong I've been and I'm truly sorry!"

Wishing to spare me from such a harsh assessment, Kanga rejected my position by offering, "You're not as bad as all that. Besides, no one else offered me a job; on account of my gender. You, Mr. Scrooge, are the only one willing to hire me. You can't be as bad as you say when you've done what no one else was willing to do."

Oddly enough, I'm ashamed by her flimsy declaration of truth. The blessing and curse with knowledge is knowing. When I know something, I know it. No attempt of pacification will alter the reality I face. I know all too well that I could have and should have done better. No matter the outcome of others, I am responsible for myself. That responsibility requires a degree of accountability which I now know falls squarely on me.

Even if I attempted to excuse myself on the standards set forth by others, I will forever know the outcome of my personal accountability. I cannot allow my fragility to be pacified based on Kanga's remark. No, I corrected her assessment by stating, "I'm afraid you're too kind."

She issued, "I'm not, I owe a great deal to you."

Embarrassed, I corrected her, "Be that as it may, I know I've been cold and unobliging. My business was to conduct business. Personal matters of warmth and understanding were never permitted. I've been callous towards you. You've worked with me for some time and I'm embarrassed to admit that I know very little about you. This simple fact is enough to condemn the worthiest of patrons, let alone a wicked sinner like me."

"Whatever do you mean?"

I concluded, "Being in the position that I'm in and yet know nothing about you indicates how selfish and unkind I've been in the manner in which I've interacted with you. For that, I am truly sorry."

As I concluded with my apology, Roo appeared. He looked as I saw him last night. Such a sweet child. Although sick, he carried such hope with him. With my eyes directed elsewhere, Kanga followed my line of sight and saw her son coming around the corner. She was equally embarrassed and nervous with the presence of Roo.

Embarrassed over what, I don't know. I could only assume it's regarding her keeping Roo from my knowledge. Her nerves, on the other hand, were another thing. It was quite clear that she feared my reaction to her having a child. In an attempt to ease her thoughts, I pried, "Who is this strapping young lad?"

Upon hearing such a declaration, Roo perked up and announced, "I'm Roo, Kanga's son. Her only son."

Roo carried himself so well. However, after exerting such efforts, the effects of being burdened with consumption for so long took hold of him. Roo coughed violently and shrunk back against the wall. Afraid of my reaction, Kanga shielded me from seeing her son's nature.

In an attempt to put her mind at ease, I inquired, "Is he okay?"

Kanga avoided answering the fullness of the matter by abbreviating the seriousness of her son's condition. She noted that it was a mild cough, one that he's been dealing with over the past week or so. She went on to note that it is likely due to the inclement weather they've been having.

The moment has arrived. The one I've been hoping for all day. At what point am I able to express the changed nature within me without any commitment of doing so. After all, it's one thing to believe in something; it's quite another to carry out that belief in those daily interactions we share with others. How can I say I'm concerned for the well-being of those around me without ever demonstrating such concerns for them.

Knowing what I know, I confidently offered, "I'm afraid I won't be needing you in the office for a while."

Kanga interrupted, "You're letting me go!"

"No, of course not. What I'm attempting to say is that it's important to me that you're here with your son, taking care of him until he is well. In fact, I'd like to cover any doctor visits which he requires."

"But sir, I can't repay you for such costs."

"There's no need to concern yourself over such matters. If it'll put your mind at rest, consider the time and delays it would cost me to replace you in the office. I highly doubt there is a soul as qualified for the position as you are. In fact, I believe you're ready to take on more responsibilities. With that comes a higher pay. There's no point in protesting this simple truth; without you, I'd be lost."

Embarrassed by my generous offer, Kanga seemed to struggle for the right words. Rather than let her stumble through some off-beat rationale, I concluded, "Kanga, I'm quite fortunate to have you work with me. Please, allow me to show it. You've earned the chance to take on further responsibilities, with that comes higher pay. In regards to your son, please take your time. Don't worry about the cost. We'll consider it as a part of your promotion. Besides, I need the best version of you and you're incapable of being that with your thoughts drawn to his well-being. When he's on the mend, feel free to bring him to the office any time you wish."

Stunned by all that has been issued, Kanga couldn't say a word. Instead, she leapt forward and embraced me. I must admit I was thrown off by her affection. It has been some time since anyone has touched me in such a way. Roo, seeing the change in his mother, hobbled towards me to thank me for what I've done.

I assured him that it was me who was the fortunate one. Roo then offered, "May God bless you Mr. Scrooge."

No one has offered me such a sentiment. If I'm not mistaken, others have preferred to ask God to curse me rather than bless me. I looked at the child and assured him that anything he needs, I'll be there.

It's been some time since that fateful Christmas Eve. I've often wondered if the experience of it was real or not. Thankfully, I've concluded that a soul can accomplish more by offering someone a jar full of honey rather than a vase full of vinegar. A bit of kindness changes the outlook far better than any sort of reproof.

Whether it was real or a dream, the effects of that night had a change on my life which cannot be denied. As the saying goes, the proof is in the pudding. With his mother by his side, Roo received the much-needed care he deserved and has since become a frequent guest of the office. I can honestly say, there is no other child who is as remarkable as he is. Seeing him grow up in the way he has, fulfilled every aspect of my life in those things that seemed to be missing.

Kanga performed so well in her duties; I had no choice but to offer her Rabbit's old position as my partner. With her, complaints are down, business is up. All of our investors couldn't be happier. She simply smooths over my rough edges. Now that I'm old and see death at my door, I can look at that day as the one which saved my life.

Whatever legacy I leave, will carry on in Roo. There can be no greater gift than the knowledge I was given, whether real or not, I know one simple truth. I love that boy! It's my belief that the love I found in him was able to spread to others. Love is what saved my soul from the misery that awaited.

Rather than dread, I'm looking forward to meeting that miserable donkey I met so many Christmases ago. I believe I'm ready. If God willing, he'll accept this wicked old sinner as a repented soul, one worthy to enter his presence. As Roo once offered me, so I offer to all, "may God bless you, everyone!"

Benjamin Egbert enjoys spending his time reading books, riding bikes, and watching movies. His hobbies involve writing and traveling. He resides with his parents and two siblings.

Michael J. Egbert started his writing career developing marketing and communication strategies for small businesses. His love for writing began at his alma mater, Utah Tech University where he studied human communication. Michael continued his education by enrolling in a master's program at the University of Southern California Annenberg, School of Communication and Journalism.

Michael is married to his college sweetheart, Delight. Together they reside in Las Vegas, Nevada, with their three children.